Space
Race

Celia Warren
Illustrated by Andy Parker

"Look at the shooting stars,"
said Space Ant.
"Wow! They are fast!"
The shooting stars zoomed across the sky.
They went fast and they went high.

"I can go faster than the shooting stars," said Elebird.

"Go on then," said Space Ant.

Elebird flew as fast as he could,
but the shooting stars went faster.

"I can jump higher than the shooting stars," said Tigeroo.

"Go on then," said Space Ant.

Tigeroo jumped as high as he could,
but the shooting stars went higher.

"I can go faster than the shooting stars,"
said Space Ant. "Come with me."
They got into the spaceship.

Up they went.
They went higher and higher.
They got closer and closer to the
shooting stars.
The shooting stars got bigger and bigger.

They raced the shooting stars.
"Faster, faster, Space Ant," said Elebird.
They went faster and faster and faster.
At last, they went faster than the stars.
whoosh!

Then Space Ant went up and over
the shooting stars.
In and out she went.
Up and down she went.

Then down and down and down they went.
Slower and slower and slower they went.
And they landed on the purple sea.